DC SUPER-PETS!™

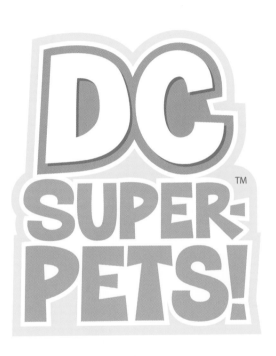

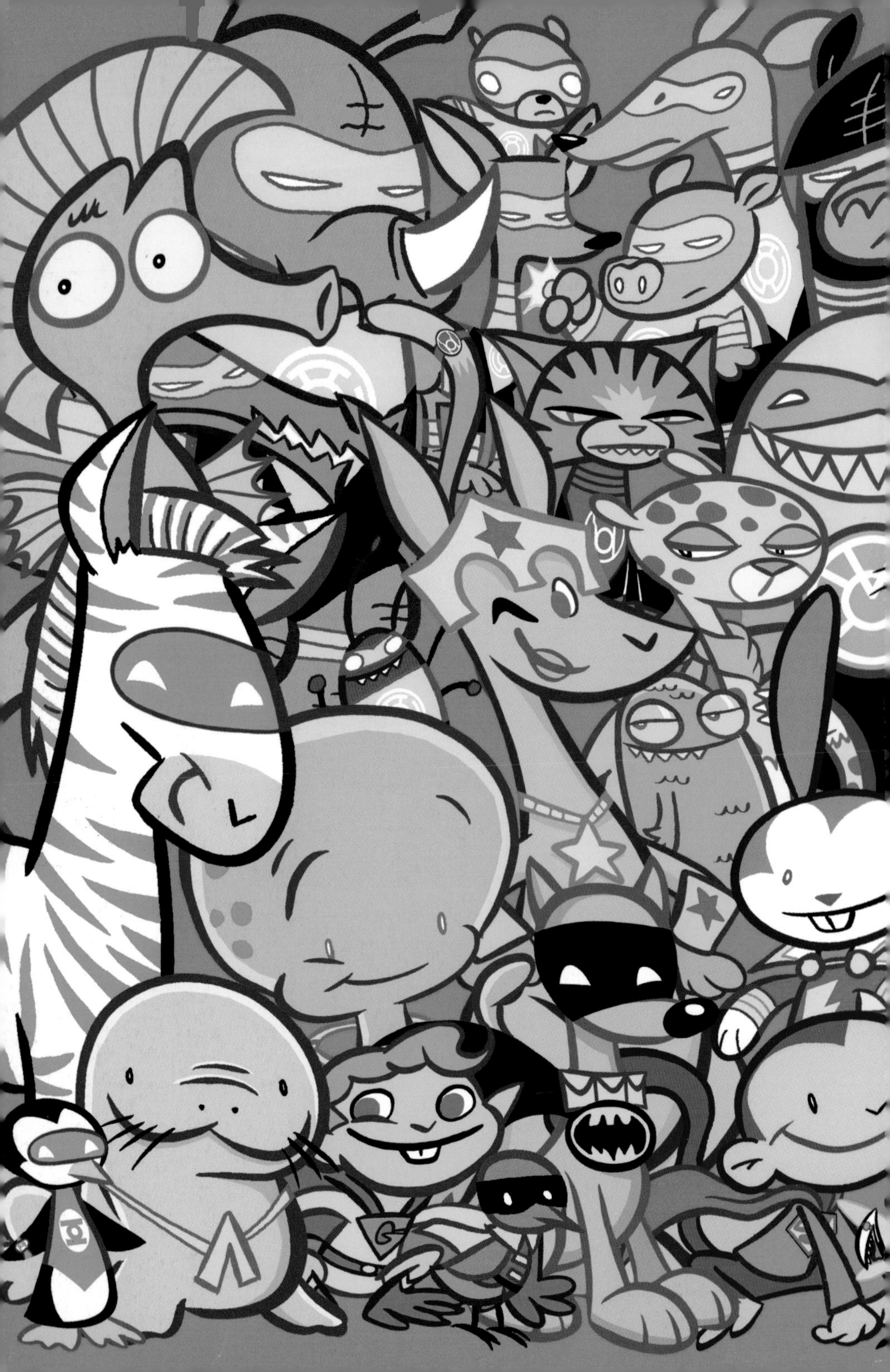

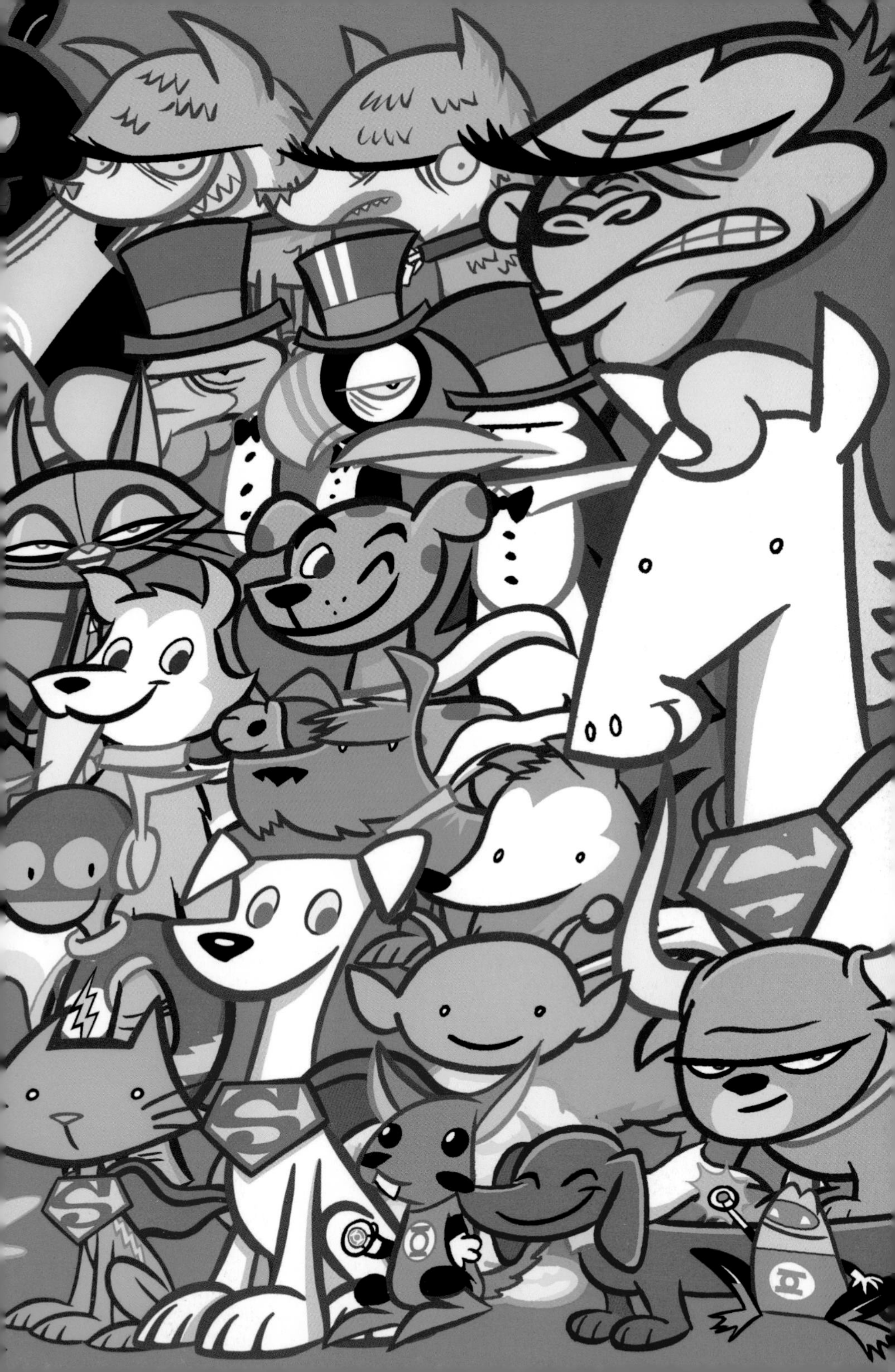

DC SUPER-PETS!™

by John
Sazaklis

ROYAL RODENT RESCUE

illustrated by
Art Baltazar

Superman created by
Jerry Siegel and Joe Shuster

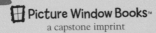
Picture Window Books™
a capstone imprint

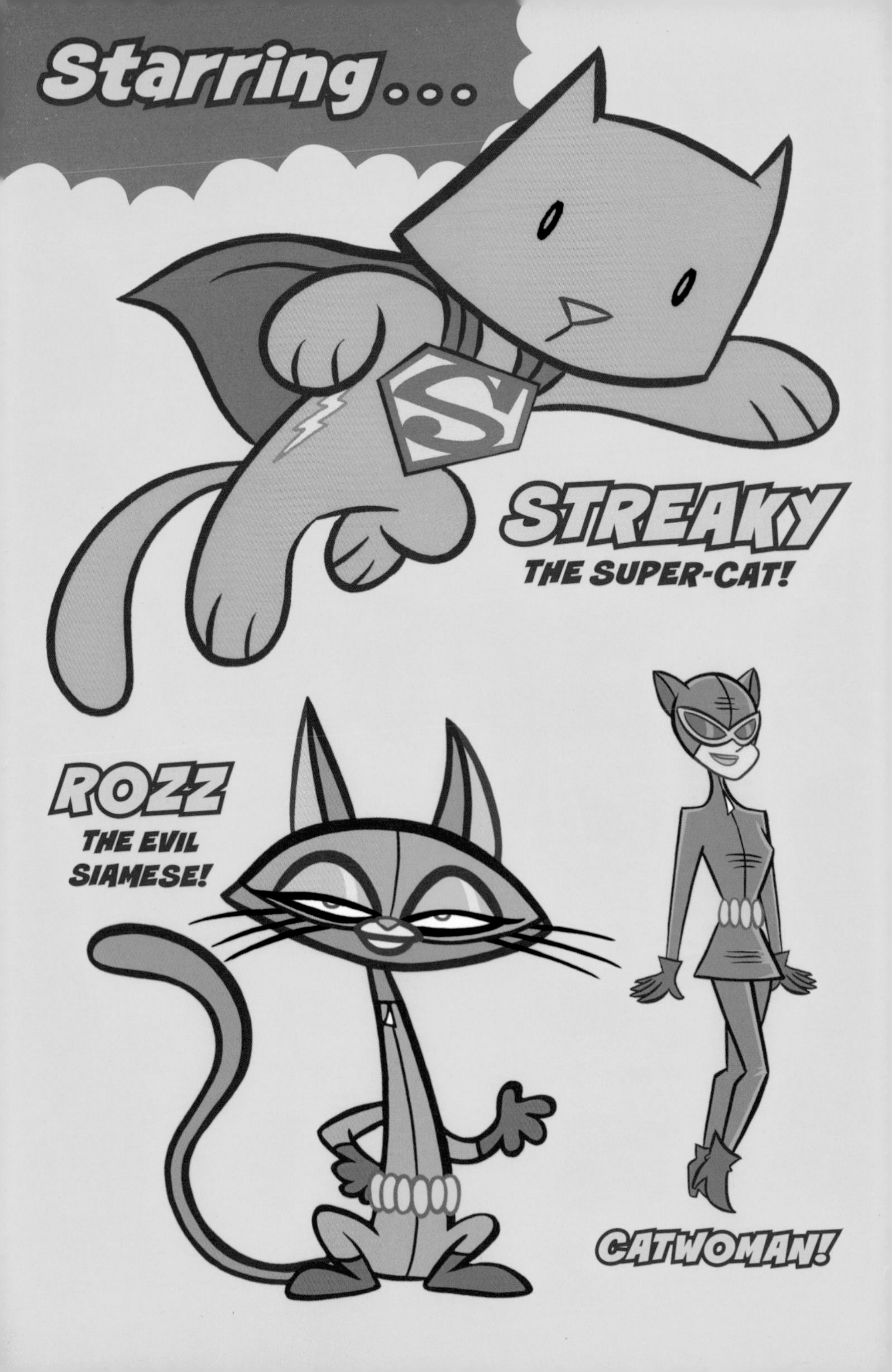
Starring...
STREAKY
THE SUPER-CAT!
ROZZ
THE EVIL SIAMESE!
CATWOMAN!

TABLE OF CONTENTS!

FORTRESS of SOLITUDE
SUPER-COMPUTER

SUPER-PET HERO FILE 004:

STREAKY

Heat Vision

X-ray Vision

Super-hearing

Super-strong Tail

Super-breath

S-shield

Lightning Bolt

Flight

Super Hero Owner:
SUPERGIRL

Species: Super-Cat

Place of birth: Earth

Age: Unknown

Favorite Foods:
Milk and sushi

Bio: While performing an experiment, Supergirl turned her pet cat into a Super-Cat! Streaky has the same powers as the Girl of Steel.

 Chapter 1

CAT OF STEEL

High above the city of Metropolis,

Streaky the Super-Cat zoomed

through the air. His super-hearing had

picked up the siren of a fire truck.

 WEEOo! WEEOo!

He followed the sound to a burning

building.

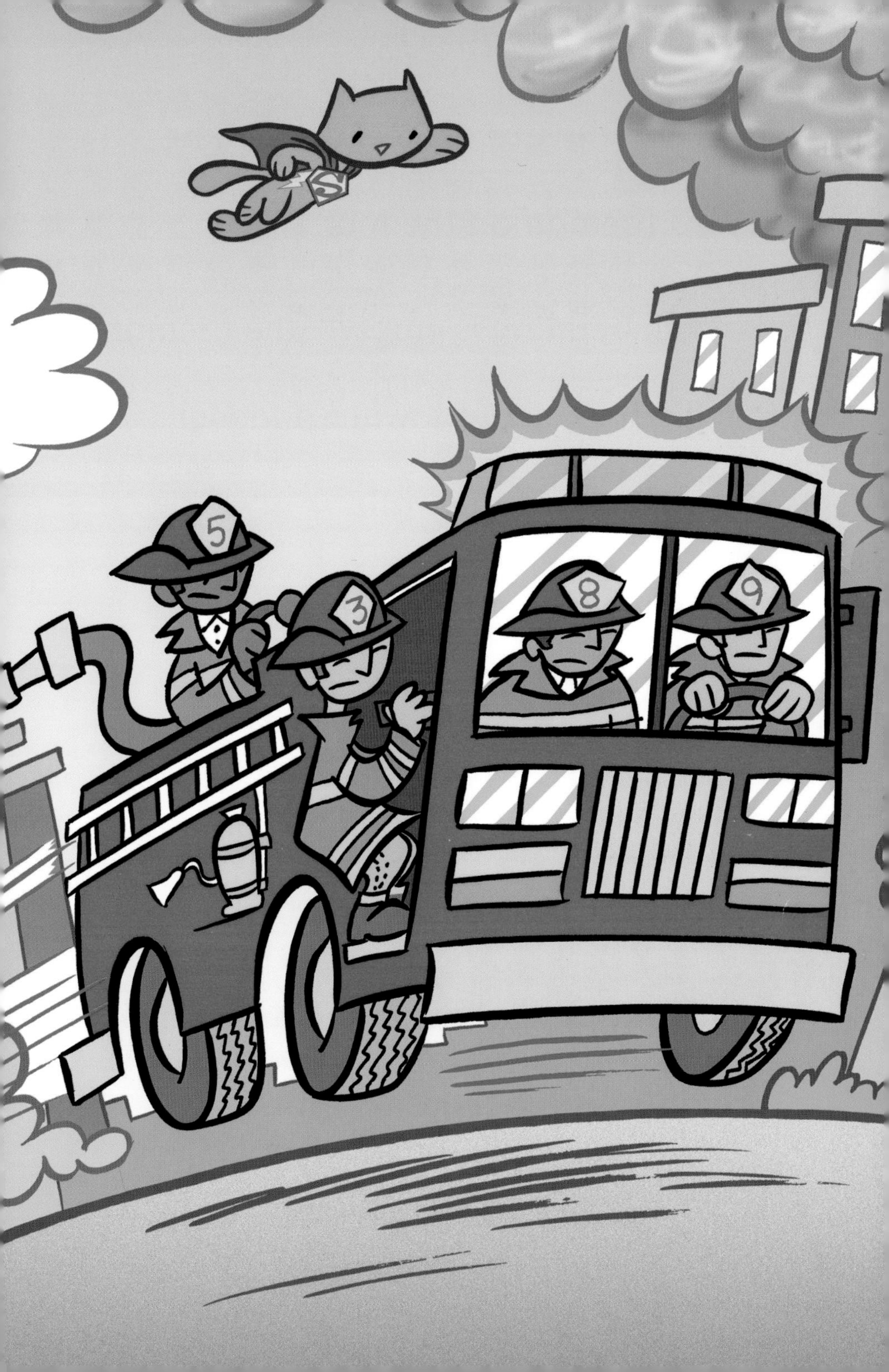
5
3
8
9

When the Cat of Steel arrived, he saw a fireman on the roof.

"The building is empty!" the fireman cried. Then he ran toward a ladder resting against the wall.

Suddenly, the fire reached a gas pipe.

The blast sent the fireman through the air. He landed in a nearby tree.

Streaky flew into the building. He used his super-breath to put out the flames. FWOOOM!

Then with his teeth, Streaky picked

up the fireman by his coat. The Super-

Cat carried him to safety.

"Would you look at that?" said the

fire chief. **"That's the first time a**

cat has gotten one of us out of

a tree!"

"HOORAY!"

The nearby crowd began to cheer.

The firemen took turns petting Streaky.

They scratched under his chin. The

feline hero purred with another job

well done.

Then Streaky flicked his tail. He

flew up, up, and away. **ZOOM!**

Soon his cape was just a red spot in

the blue sky.

Reaching the **Fortress of Solitude,**

Streaky let out a deep breath.

"All that hero work is tiring,"
Streaky said. "And you know what
that means? **It's time for a nap!**"

Streaky
curled up in a
special part of
the Fortress. His

owner, Supergirl, had made the spot
just for him. After cleaning his fur,
Streaky closed his eyes. He fell asleep.

BWEE-OO! BWEE-OO!

An alarm rang through the Fortress
of Solitude.

Streaky leaped out of bed and into

the air. He held on to the icy ceiling

with his claws.

"**What is going on?**" Streaky cried.

The Super-Cat flew toward a computer in the main room of the Fortress. He rubbed his eyes. On the screen was a live shot of Metropolis. The giant robot villain Metallo was smashing through the city.

Streaky fixed his red cape. He headed for the exit. Then the image on the computer changed. Supergirl appeared. The Girl of Steel was fighting the robot.

"That's more like it!" Streaky said. The cat headed back to bed.

In Gotham City, **Rozz the Siamese cat** paced around a hideout. Her owner, the evil **Catwoman**, looked at stolen jewelry in a mirror.

On most days, Rozz would help Catwoman with crimes. Today, Batgirl was searching for them. They had to stay hidden. Rozz was getting really bored.

Catwoman turned on the TV to see if her robbery had made the news. Instead, she saw the video of Supergirl fighting Metallo in Metropolis.

Suddenly, a great shadow filled the screen. It was the shadow of the Batplane!

Batgirl had come to help her super-

hero friend. Together, the World's

Finest Heroes stopped the robot

monster!

"With Batgirl in Metropolis,

Gotham City is mine for the taking,"

Catwoman said. She jumped onto the

window ledge. "When the Bat's away,

this Cat will play!"

The villain leaped from the window.

She fled into the night.

Rozz was excited by what she saw on TV. A whole new city was out there to explore. She packed a bag and put it over her shoulder. Then she left the hideout and headed to the bus stop. **Rozz was going to Metropolis!**

Chapter 2

CAT BURGLAR

Soon the bus reached the city. Rozz hopped off. She had been hiding in the space for luggage.

As she stretched her legs, Rozz took in the sights. Unlike Gotham City, Metropolis was shiny and clean. It looked brand new. **PURRR!**

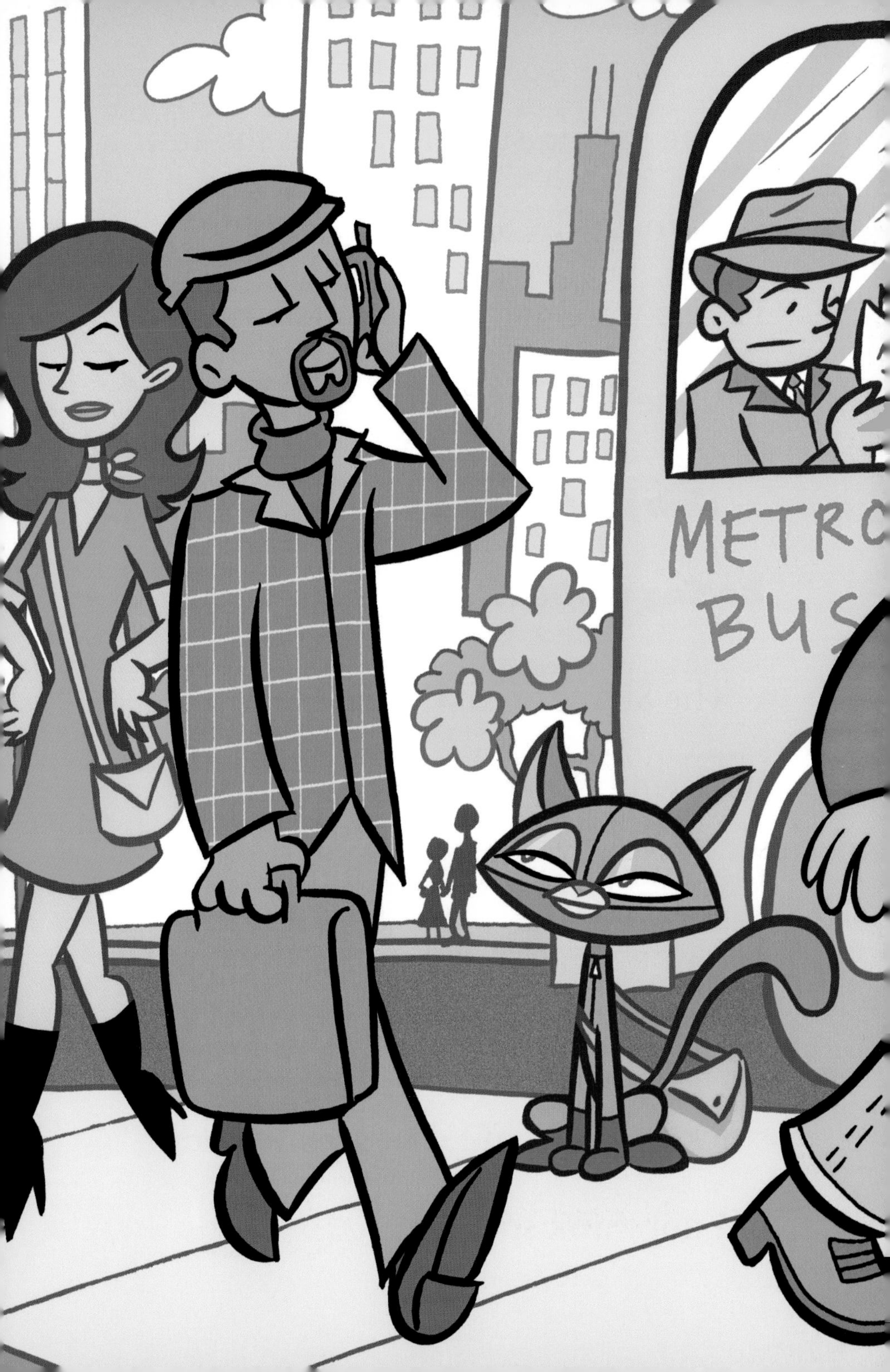
METRO
BUS

The setting sun glowed on the tall buildings. The shops were closing. People were going home. The city became calm and quiet.

This place is pretty boring without crime, Rozz thought.

The Siamese cat decided to make her own fun. Rozz hopped onto the fence of a nearby building. She began to sing. She thought she had a lovely singing voice. The man who stuck his head out a nearby window did not think so.

 he shouted.

"Tough crowd," Rozz said to herself. She sang louder.

"Scat, cat!" the man yelled. He threw a shoe at Rozz.

The shoe whizzed past her head. It smashed through the window of an electronics store. The alarm sounded. The man gasped. He shut his window and turned off the lights.

"That's my signal to leave!" Rozz said. She ran down the alley.

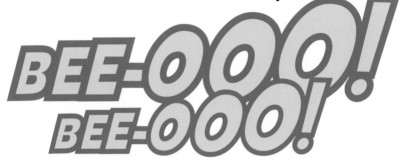

Another alarm sounded in the Fortress of Solitude. Streaky got up and rubbed his eyes. A break-in at an electronics store. He knew it was his turn to save the day.

When Streaky got to the store, the owner was holding a shoe. He was talking to Police Officer Merkel.

"Nothing was stolen, officer," said the store owner. "But my window is broken."

"We'll find the criminal," replied Officer Merkel. "No need to worry."

Streaky saw that everything was under control. He curled up on top of a TV. The Super-Cat continued his nap. If he was needed, he'd be close by to help.

Meanwhile, Rozz searched for a place to spend the night. She came upon the Harper Hotel. The hotel had marble steps and a fancy fountain.

"This will do!" Rozz said to herself.

In front of the hotel, a limo pulled up. Rozz hid behind a step and watched. Several photographers ran out of the hotel. Camera flashes lit up the sky as the passengers stepped out of the car. Dressed in red robes, King Sandy and Queen Markela of Kardamyla greeted the crowd.

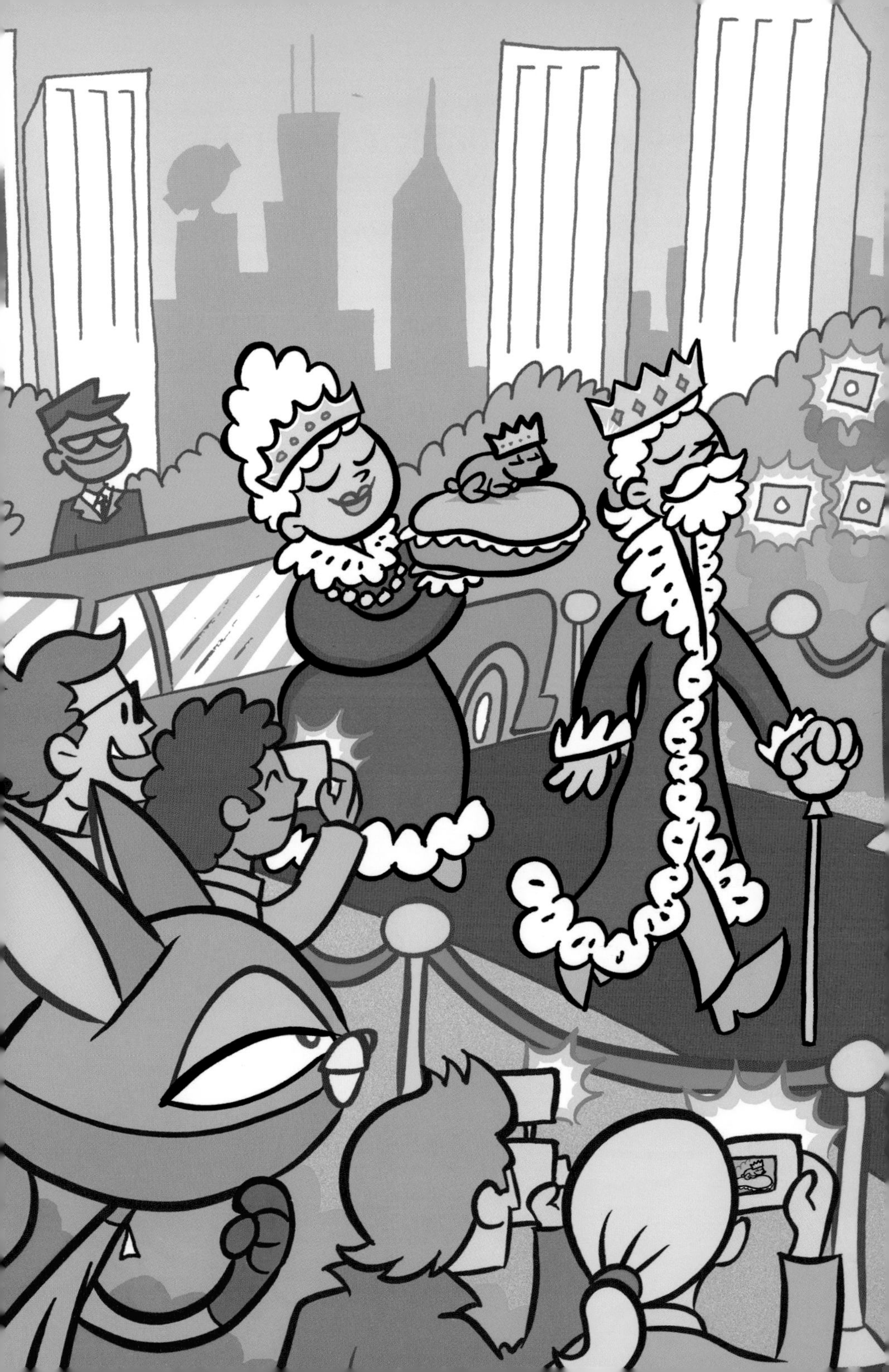

As the royal family entered the hotel, Rozz saw the queen carrying a pillow. A ball of brown fur sat on top. It was the queen's hamster, Prince Zouli. He was sound asleep.

Rozz's eyes widened.

MEOWW!!!

"That royal rodent will fetch me a king's ransom!" Rozz said.

Everyone knew Queen Markela's riches came from the trees found on her island. Their sweet sap was used to make many products, such as soap, lotion, and toothpaste. It was also used to make chewing gum, bread, and sweet treats.

Rozz had only dreamed of such gifts. Her stomach rumbled at the thought.

Rozz hurried into the hotel. A group of waiters and bellhops followed the royal family. They were carrying luggage and pushing food carts.

Rozz hopped on a passing food cart. She enjoyed the ride. **She would soon have her paws on Prince Zouli!**

A few hours later, the king and queen were asleep. Prince Zouli the hamster didn't sleep at night. Instead, he headed toward the food cart. The prince climbed up the cart to a tray of cheese.

Suddenly, he was snatched by a powerful set of claws! Rozz dropped Zouli into her bag. She climbed down the fire escape.

The hotel would soon be filled with police.

Once Rozz was on the street, something caught her eye. Next to the hotel was the perfect place to hide — **Papa Duke's Pet Shop!** Rozz found her way in. She locked up the prince in an empty birdcage. She smiled.

"You'll never get away with this!" squeaked Prince Zouli. "The pets of my country will come to Metropolis! They'll make you pay!"

"Relax, rat," hissed Rozz. She flashed her claws at the poor little hamster. **"Or else!!"**

RODENT RESCUE

The next day, Streaky was startled

awake once again. He looked up from

his napping place in the electronics

store. A crowd of worried shoppers

stood around the wall of television sets.

Each TV was tuned to the WKAT News

channel.

On each screen, an image of King Sandy and Queen Markela appeared. They looked upset. Their pet hamster, Prince Zouli, had been taken in the night.

Suddenly, a Siamese cat hopped onto the news desk. The cat looked toward the cameras. She meowed and waved her paws wildly.

"Meoww!! Meowww!!"

Humans couldn't understand the evil feline. But Streaky heard the message loud and clear.

"**Pets of Metropolis,**" said the cat on screen. "**My name is Rozz. These are my demands!**"

Rozz asked for a large amount of gifts. She wanted a lifetime supply of treats from the royal family's island.

Rozz was planning to steal from Zouli's kingdom! Streaky had to find the hamster prince. He had to stop this crazy cat.

Using his super-hearing, the Cat of Steel picked up the signal from the TV station. Streaky zoomed into the sky. He followed it.

The Super-Cat blasted into the news station. As the dust cleared, Streaky landed proudly on the news desk.

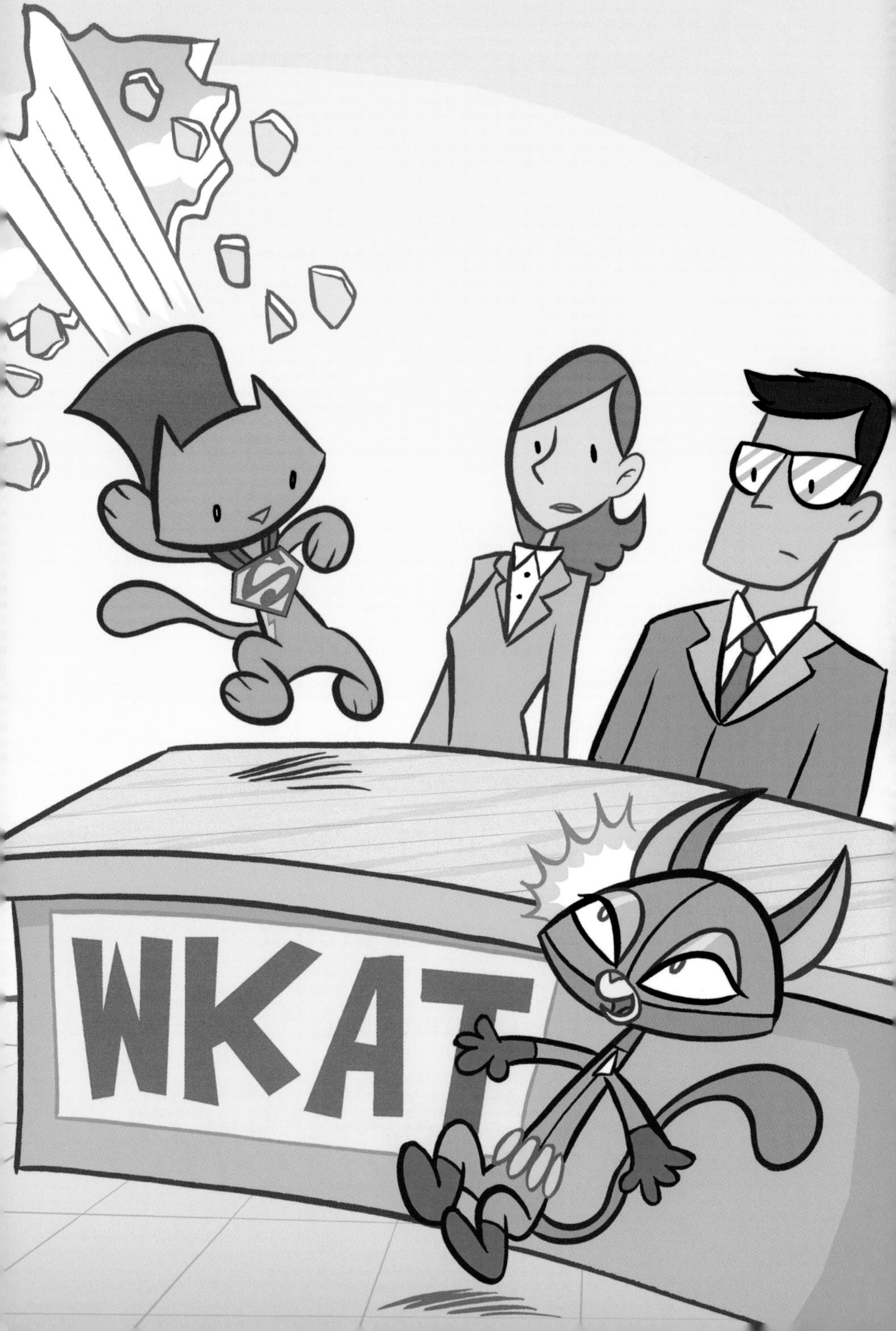
WKAT

"Show's over, Rozz!" shouted Streaky.

"You must belong to Supergirl," said Rozz. "The hero of Metropolis."

"That's right," said Streaky. "Now tell me where the prince is located. We'll settle this quietly."

"I don't think so," purred the Siamese. **"The fun has just begun!"**

Rozz reached into her bag. She pulled out a collar. Dangling from it was a glowing piece of green rock.

Kryptonite!!

Rozz held the collar toward Streaky.
The green rock made the Super-Cat's
powers weak.

"I work for Catwoman. She has evil

friends," said Rozz. "That's how I got

my paws on this rock."

"I suggest you keep your distance, Super-Cat," Rozz laughed. **"You're looking a little green."**

Rozz hopped off the desk. Streaky was too weak to chase her. The Siamese cat burglar leaped through the hole in the wall. She was gone.

Moments later, Streaky's strength returned. He flew out of the TV station. Rozz was nowhere to be found. The Cat of Steel used his super-smelling to pick up the villain's scent. He followed the trail to Papa Duke's Pet Shop.

Streaky climbed into an air vent.

Using his X-ray vision, he looked

through the metal vent and into the

store. Across the room, Prince Zouli

was locked in a birdcage. Directly

underneath, Rozz sat atop a large fish

tank. She was looking for a snack.

The Super-Cat acted fast. He aimed

his heat vision toward the cage. He

blasted two energy beams at the lock.

ZAPPP! ZAPPP!

The cage door flew open. Then the

royal rodent made a run for it.

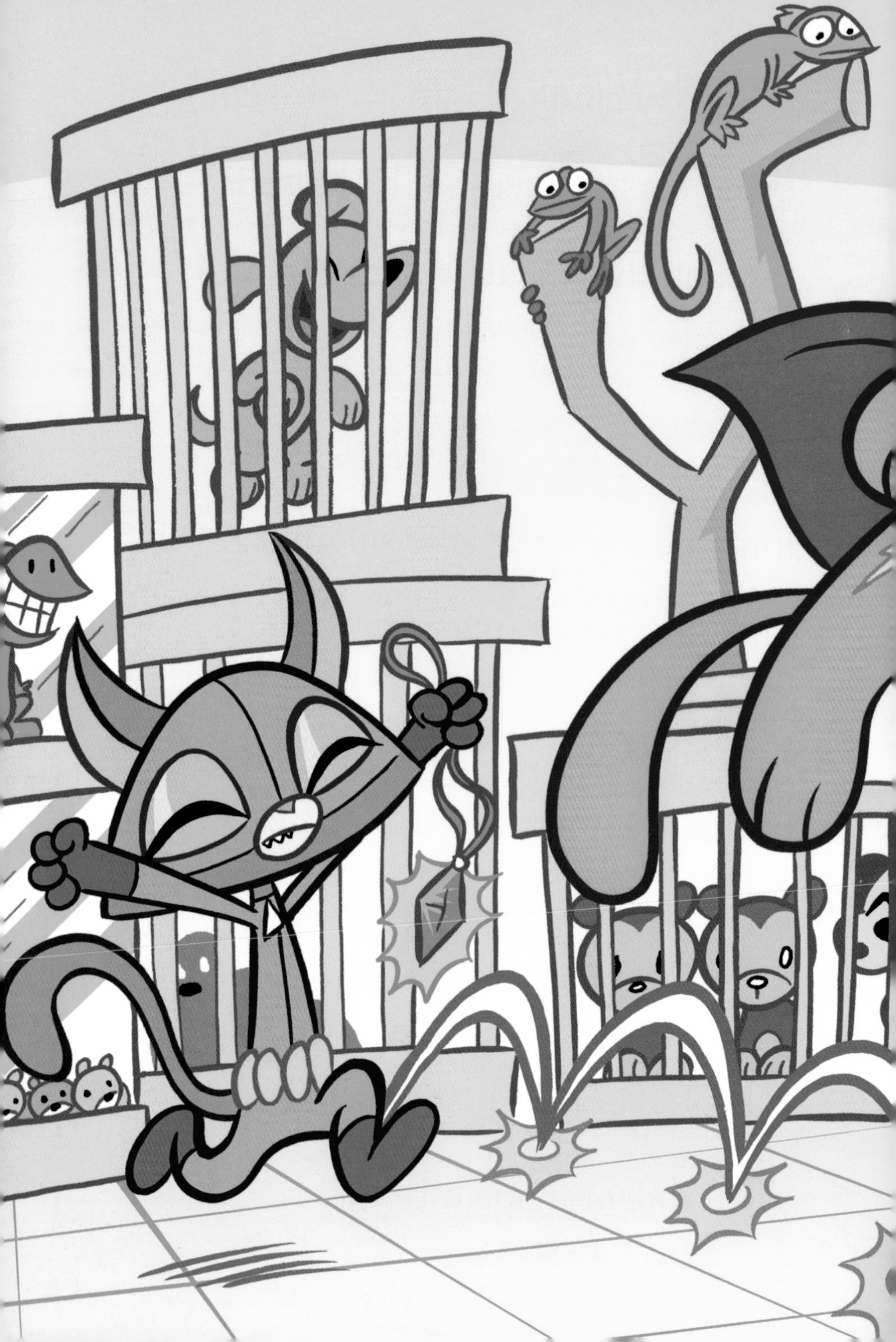

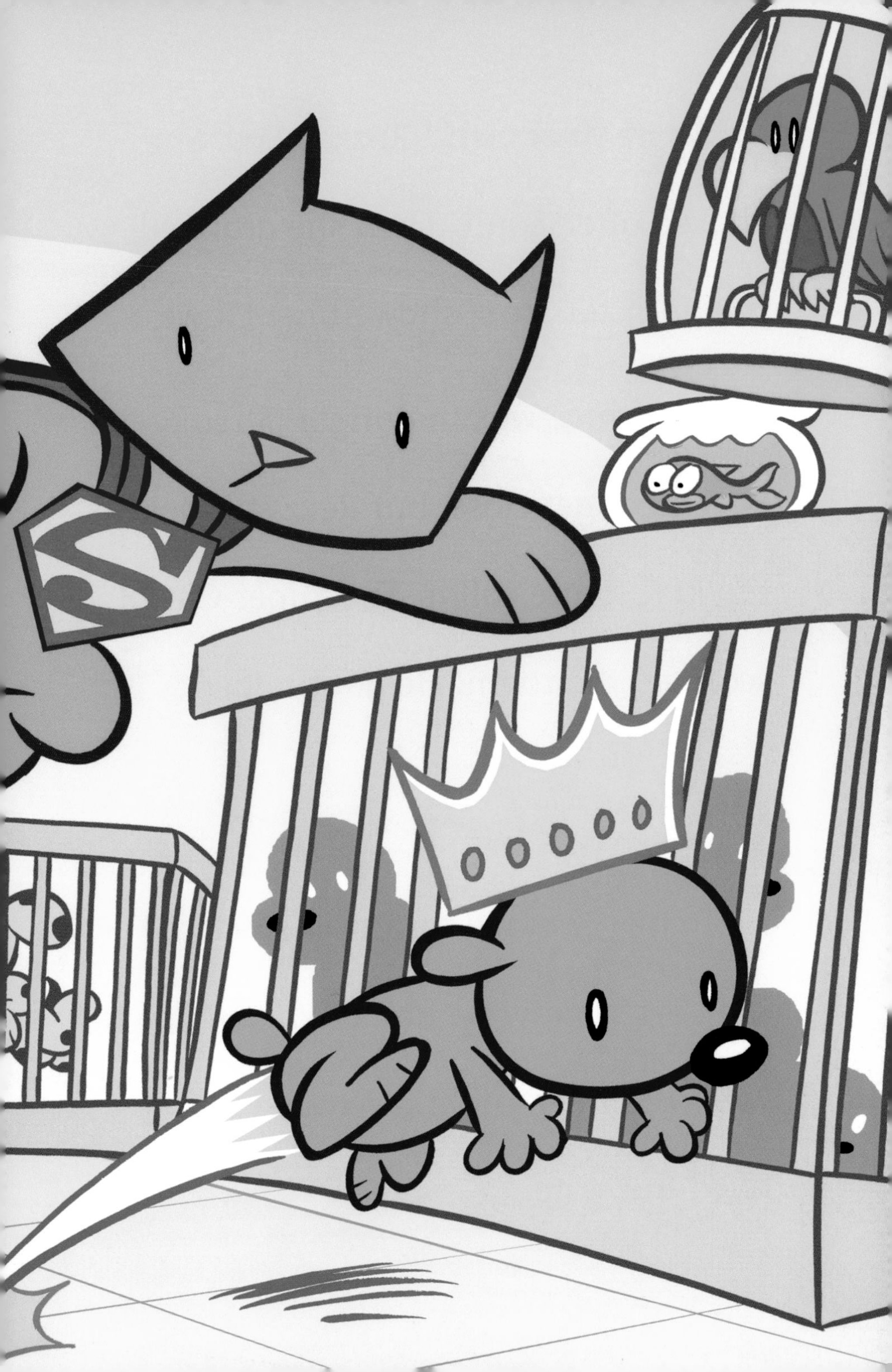

"Drat that rat!" Rozz yelled. She chased after Zouli. Then she grabbed the hamster. Rozz showed her claws.

The prince was in danger! Streaky needed to get close, but Rozz still held the kryptonite collar. The Super-Cat scanned the room. He got an idea.

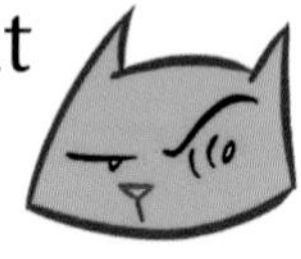

WOOOOSH!

Streaky zoomed toward a stack of kitty litter bags. He landed on them with all of his might. A cloud of dust filled the store.

Rozz dropped Zouli. She turned

toward Streaky and hissed.

"You sure like to make an entrance,

Super-Cat," Rozz said. **"Now it's time**

to make your exit!" The evil feline

leaped onto the Cat of Steel.

The kryptonite collar was too much for Streaky. He started to black out.

Prince Zouli knew the collar was hurting Streaky. He raced up to Rozz. He grabbed the collar with his little paws. Using his sharp teeth, Zouli bit through the strap.

MUNCH! MUNCH! MUNCH!

The collar fell out of Rozz's grasp. The hamster ran with it toward the exit. He squeezed under the door and into the street. Once outside, Zouli dropped the collar down a sewer drain.

Streaky's powers returned. In a flash, Rozz found herself inside the empty birdcage. Streaky bent the bars shut around her. She was trapped.

"Looks like your criminal career is for the birds," Streaky said to Rozz.

Streaky turned to Prince Zouli. "Thanks for your help, your majesty," he said to the hamster prince.

"I was only returning the favor, dear friend," Prince Zouli replied.

Streaky put Prince Zouli on his back. He flew the royal hamster back to the hotel. The king and queen were overjoyed at the return of their pet. They showered Streaky with gifts.

Streaky curled up on the king's pillow. **A nap was the best gift of all.**

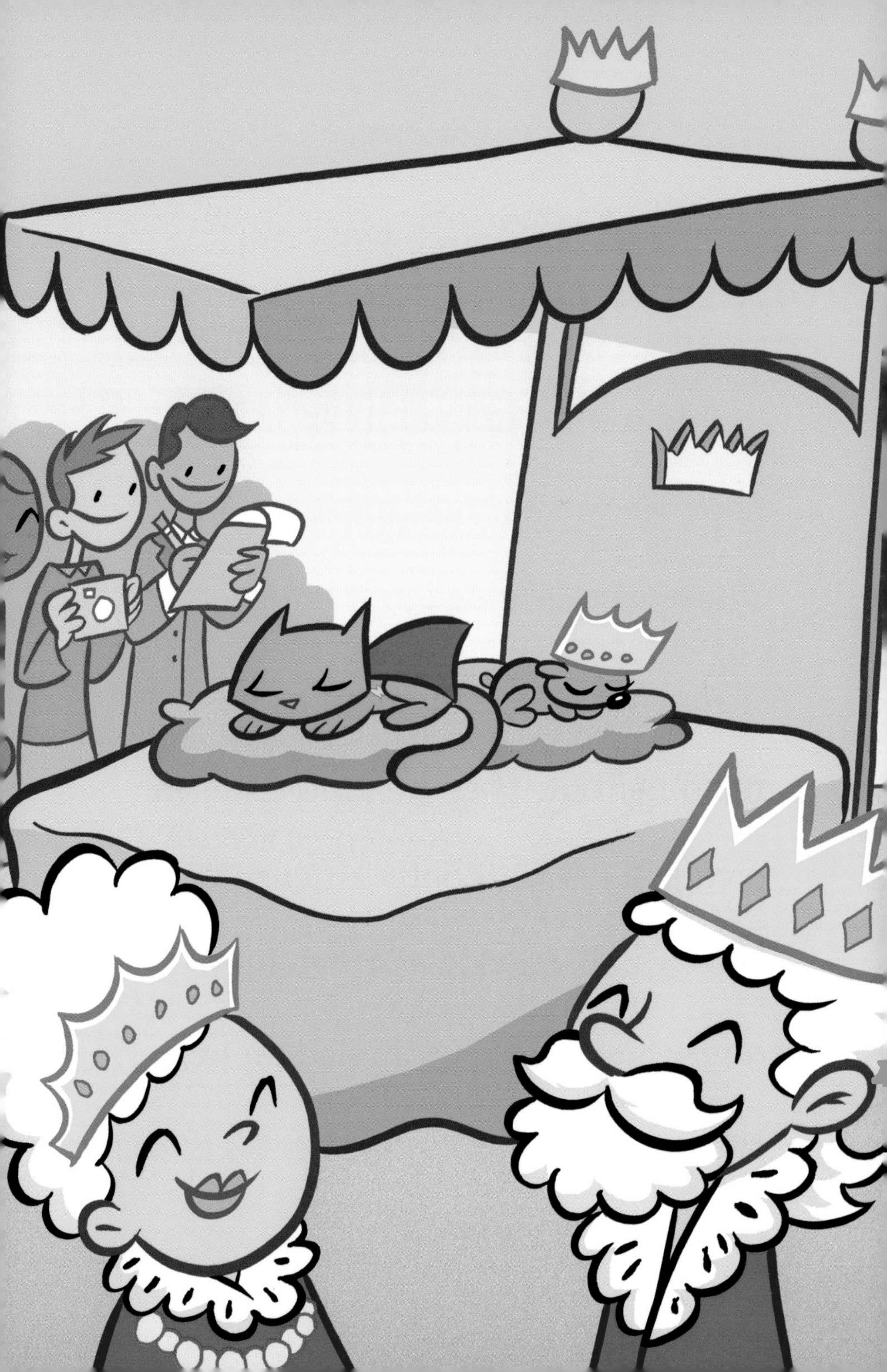

* * *

The next morning, Papa Duke opened his pet shop. He was surprised to find a mess of kitty litter on the floor. He was more surprised to find a Siamese cat trapped in a birdcage.

Rozz clawed at the man as he lifted her out. Then he placed her in a cage filled with baby kittens. The cute critters quickly warmed up to the angry Siamese. They pulled on her ears. They climbed on her back. Rozz could hardly stand it.

"Well, you wanted excitement," Rozz said to herself. **"Try getting yourself out of this one."**

KNOW YOUR

Krypto

Streaky

Beppo

Comet

Ace

Jumpa

Whatzit

B'dg

Storm

Topo

Ark

Hoppy

Paw Pooch

Bull Dog

Chameleon Collie

Hot Dog

Aw yeah,
HERO
PETS!

Tail Terrier

Tusky Husky

SUPER-PETS!

Ignatius

Chauncey

Crackers

Giggles

Artie Puffin

Griff

Waddles

Rozz

Dex-Starr

Glomulus

Misty

Sneezers

Whoosh

Pronto

Snorrt

Rolf

Squealer

Kajunn

AW YEAH, JOKES!

What do cats eat for breakfast?

What?!

Mice Crispies!

Do you know why cats aren't good storytellers?

Why?

They only have one tail!

Why did the cat get a computer?

Dunno.

So he could have his very own mouse!

bellhop (BEL-hop)—a hotel employee who helps guests with their luggage

burglar (BURG-lur)—someone who steals things

electronics (i-lek-TRON-iks)—devices powered by electricity, such as computers, TVs, and radios

Fortress of Solitude (FOR-triss UHV SAHL-uh-tood)—the secret headquarters of Supergirl

ransom (RAN-suhm)—money being demanded before someone being held can be set free

Siamese cat (sye-uh-MEEZ CAT)—a slender breed of cat with short hair and a pale brown or gray coat; its ears, paws, and tail are often dark.

villain (VIL-uhn)—an evil person or animal

WORD POWER!

MEET THE AUTHOR!

John Sazaklis

John Sazaklis spent part of life working in a family coffee shop, the House of Donuts. The other part, he spent drawing and writing stories. He has illustrated Spider-Man books and written Batman books for HarperCollins. He has also created toys used in *MAD Magazine.* John lives in Astoria, New York.

MEET THE ILLUSTRATOR!

Eisner Award-winner Art Baltazar

Art Baltazar is a cartoonist machine from the heart of Chicago! He defines cartoons and comics not only as an art style, but as a way of life. Currently, Art is the creative force behind *The New York Times* best-selling, Eisner Award-winning, DC Comics series Tiny Titans and the co-writer for *Billy Batson and the Magic of SHAZAM!* Art is living the dream! He draws comics and never has to leave the house. He lives with his lovely wife, Rose, big boy Sonny, little boy Gordon, and little girl Audrey. Right on!

READ THEM ALL!

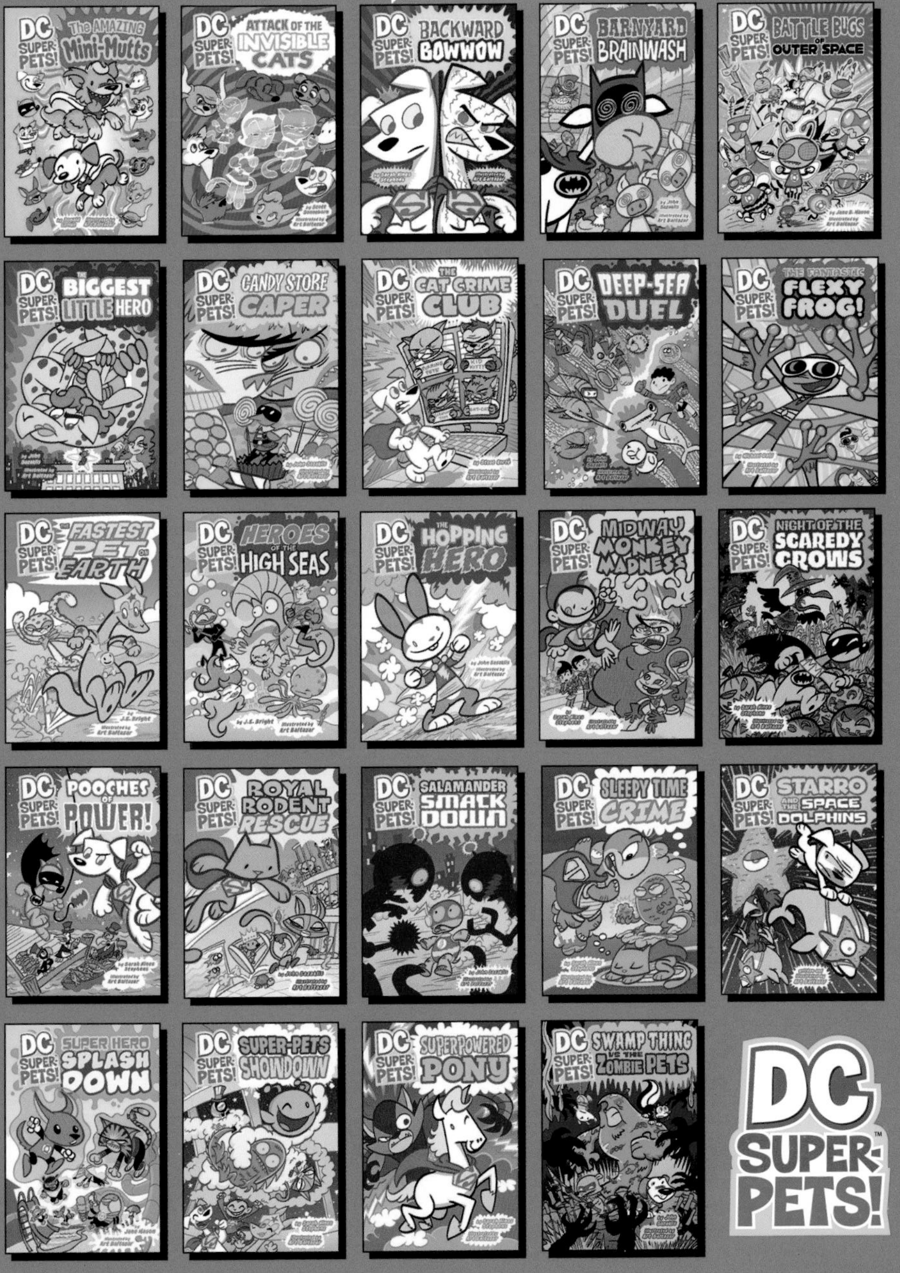
DC SUPER-PETS! The Amazing Mini-Mutts
DC SUPER-PETS! Attack of the Invisible Cats
DC SUPER-PETS! Backward Bowwow
DC SUPER-PETS! Barnyard Brainwash
DC SUPER-PETS! Battle Bugs of Outer Space
DC SUPER-PETS! The Biggest Little Hero
DC SUPER-PETS! Candy Store Caper
DC SUPER-PETS! The Cat Crime Club
DC SUPER-PETS! Deep-Sea Duel
DC SUPER-PETS! The Fantastic Flexy Frog!
DC SUPER-PETS! The Fastest Pet on Earth
DC SUPER-PETS! Heroes of the High Seas
DC SUPER-PETS! The Hopping Hero
DC SUPER-PETS! Midway Monkey Madness
DC SUPER-PETS! Night of the Scaredy Crows
DC SUPER-PETS! Pooches of Power!
DC SUPER-PETS! Royal Rodent Rescue
DC SUPER-PETS! Salamander Smack Down
DC SUPER-PETS! Sleepy Time Crime
DC SUPER-PETS! Starro and the Space Dolphins
DC SUPER-PETS! Super Hero Splash Down
DC SUPER-PETS! Super-Pets Showdown
DC SUPER-PETS! Superpowered Pony
DC SUPER-PETS! Swamp Thing vs the Zombie Pets

DC SUPER-PETS!™

THE FUN DOESN'T STOP HERE!

Discover more:

- Videos & Contests!
- Games & Puzzles!
- Heroes & Villains!
- Authors & Illustrators!

@ www.capstonekids.com

Find cool websites and more books like this one at www.facthound.com Just type in Book I.D. 9781404863071 and you're ready to go!

Picture Window Books™

Published in 2011
A Capstone Imprint
1710 Roe Crest Drive
North Mankato, Minnesota 56003
www.capstonepub.com

Copyright © 2013 DC Comics.
All related characters and elements are trademarks of and © DC Comics.
(s13)

STAR13267

Cataloging-in-Publication Data is available at the Library of Congress website.
ISBN: 978-1-4048-6307-1 (library binding)
ISBN: 978-1-4048-6622-5 (paperback)

Summary: The evil Siamese cat Rozz has kidnapped a royal hamster. Luckily, Streaky the Super-Cat is on the case! But when Rozz wears kryptonite in her collar, the Cat of Steel must find a way to rescue the rodent and save himself as well.

Art Director & Designer: Bob Lentz
Editor: Donald Lemke
Creative Director: Heather Kindseth
Editorial Director: Michael Dahl

Printed in the United States of America in North Mankato, Minnesota.
052016   009789R

DC SUPER-PETS!

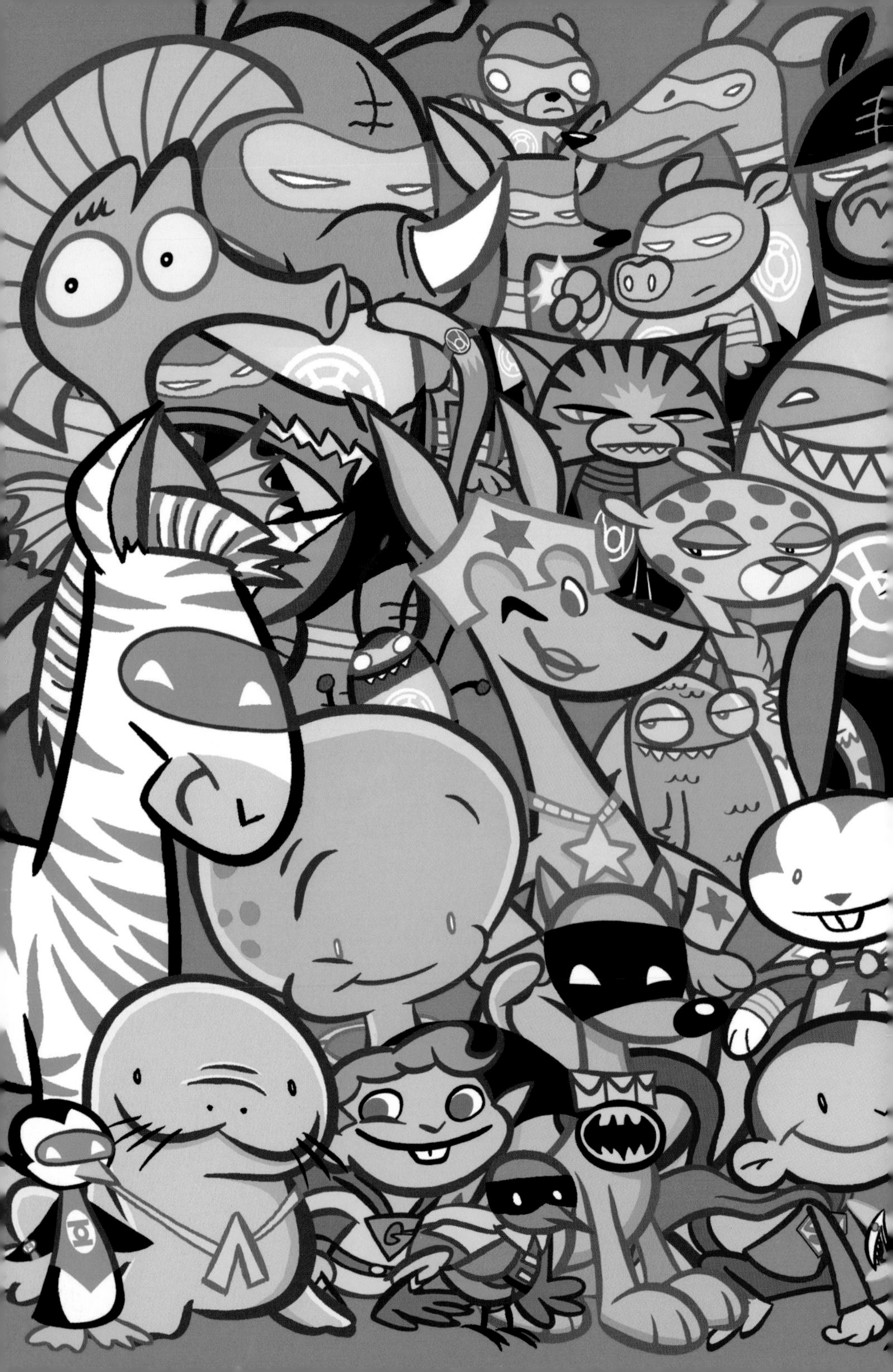

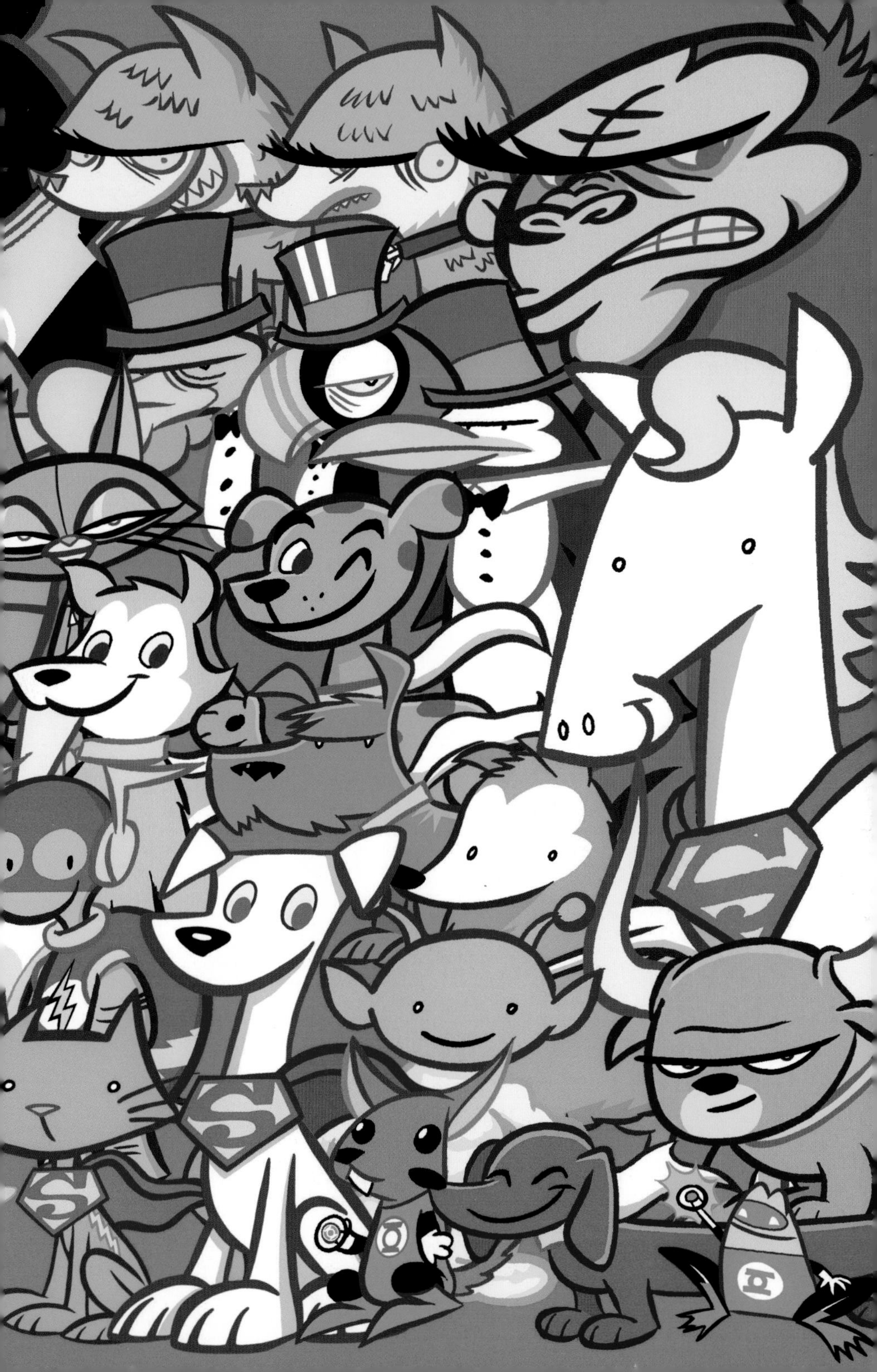

DC SUPER-PETS!™

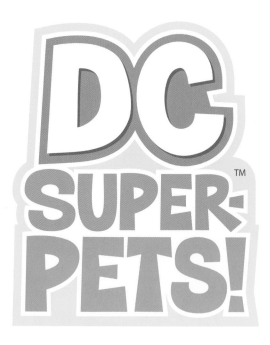